The Bitter Fruit
of Forever

JACKIE FUCHS

FOR THE SURVIVORS

1

Soo-zee Wanabi stood on his hind legs and scanned the forest, feeling exposed in his old skin. Royal soldiers could be anywhere. Soo-zee wouldn't feel safe until he had shed and gone back to being his usual, plain brown self.

He brought the intertalker to his mouth. "Zone two, confirm antenna in position," he chirped. It was time for the nightly broadcast of His Grace, supreme leader of the burrow colonies and 105th hereditary overlord of the Now World.

He wished Cho-ahn Worushi, the squad's codebreaker, had returned from his mission. He'd been gone for over half a moon now and Soo-zee missed his enthusiasm, the way his pink crest bristled with excitement whenever he cracked His Grace's code. "I've got it, Wanabi," Cho-ahn would chirp in triumph. Then they would celebrate with a coupling, a bonding as much spiritual as physical. Until Cho-ahn returned, it was Soo-zee's job to listen to the nightly royal broadcast and report on it. But when it came to breaking the coded portion, he was as helpless as a hatchling. Even Cho-ahn had trouble deciphering more than a phrase or two most nights.

The intertalker crackled. "It's already in place, Soo-zee," Roh-kee Kazeyo chirped back.

Soo-zee's crest twitched with annoyance. How many times had he told Roh-kee not to use real names over the intertalker? But Soo-zee had no right to rebuke him. Roh-kee and his burrow brother, Roh-koh Onono, were the squad's dominant members. Until he could defeat them in claw-to-claw combat, he would continue to bob his head to them. At least they had never demanded his hindquarters.

Soo-zee turned on the receiver. The address had already commenced. Soo-zee half listened as His Grace berated the rebels with his usual insults: they were heathens who didn't believe in the Iridescent Spirit; they were murderers, traitors, and thieves. He had heard it a hundred times before, yet his crest still bristled when His Grace called them "cannibals." It was true that a group of rebel soldiers had resorted to eating hatchlings during the Long Burrows Siege. But they had been speckled meat-eaters like the Rohs. Most soldiers would never dream of eating the flesh of anything other than insects, let alone their own kind.

His Grace's litany ended. It was time for the executions, the part Soo-zee dreaded. Enemies real and imagined followed His Grace as surely as the shedding of old skin followed the dinka dinka harvest. As much as he hated it, Soo-zee forced himself to listen every time the condemned confessed and were burned alive. It reminded him what they were fighting for.

The announcer could barely conceal his excitement as he chirped the names of those slated for the fire. The night's executions were to include one of His Grace's most trusted advisors — his sixth wife's brother, who had dared to question the conscription of juveniles into the royal army.

There was a chittering of nervous anticipation as His Grace's honor guard escorted the royal brother-in-law to the stake. It almost drowned out the next name: Cho-ahn Worushi. Soo-zee gasped. His Grace had never burned a juvenile before. There must be some mistake. Surely they didn't mean to kill Cho-ahn.

The announcer finished chirping the names on the death list. The hush that followed was so complete Soo-zee could hear the flames crackling in the background. He imagined the army storming into Burrow Town and rescuing his friend. But they would never risk so much for a mere novice, not even one with as much promise as Cho-ahn.

One by one the alleged traitors confessed. Then the death cries started, a shrieking that made the tips of Soo-zee's crest ripple from head to tail and back again. He imagined Cho-ahn's lovely pink scales turning black in the fire, Cho-ahn calling his name as he died. He lashed his tail against the tree trunk, cursing the Iridescent Spirit for allowing a tyrant like His Grace to rule.

Soo-zee wondered why their camp leader, Bah-Kah Takebi, had sent a novice on a such an obviously dangerous mission. He concentrated on His Grace's squealing to see if there might be some clue in it, but couldn't decipher a word. With Cho-ahn gone, the squad would need a new code breaker. Learning to break code required time, however. And no one with aptitude was interested in joining an inexperienced squad led by a freak like Bah-kah, a long, skinny orange with a yellow streak down his tail.

Maybe the Rohs were right and His Grace was mad as a sparkbug, his squealing nothing more than the ravings of a deranged mind. The squad's scout, Little Dinka, on the other hand, believed His Grace's messages were intended for Night Slayers, the elite royal assassins of legend who painted their scales as purple as midnight. Little Dinka was obsessed with Slayers. He loved to regale the others with tales of companies that had been infiltrated by one, stories that inevitably ended with some hapless soldier waking in the morning to find a severed tail twitching in his nest dripping green blood and goo.

Little Dinka's stories gave the rest of the squad

nightmares. The slightest sound would spook them: a snapping twig, the wind rustling the undergrowth, a pair of soldiers grunting as they coupled elsewhere in the burrow. The next morning they would drag their tails to the drill yard almost as late as Little Dinka. They would make mistakes that infuriated Bah-kah.

"Think with your heads, not your hindquarters," Bah-kah would hiss, his yellow-streaked tail whipping back and forth. His second-in-command, Goo-nah Kisasu, would follow closely behind him, agreeing with everything Bah-kah chirped and doling out punishment on his behalf with a switch.

"There is no such thing as Night Slayers," Bah-kah would hiss. *Thwack* would go Goo-nah's switch. "That is only what His Disgrace wants you to believe." *Thwack thwack.* "*I*, Bah-kah Takebi, will tell you what is real." *Thwack.* "*I* will show what you should be scared of." *Thwack thwack thwack.*

The sun dropped low in the sky. Overhead, the canopy purpled. The receiver fell quiet and Soo-zee looked for Little Dinka, who was due to relieve Soo-zee on watch but was, as usual, running late. By the time Soo-zee spotted his silver crest weaving through the underbrush, the first stars had appeared in the sky, a dangerous time for someone with Little Dinka's coloring to be on the move. While Little Dinka was mostly as brown as Soo-Zee, his crest was as pale as the dinka dinka plant at harvest time, when the leaves faded to white and the fragrant blue seeds were ready for picking. It was lighter even than Cho-ahn's had been, a fact Little Dinka had known would entice Soo-zee when he'd first presented him with his hindquarters not a triday after Cho-ahn had left on his mission. Little Dinka should have camouflaged his crest for night watch, but he was overly proud of his appearance. Soo-zee only hoped it wouldn't get them killed someday.

"Evening, Wanabi," Little Dinka chirped softly from below. He was the only one other than Cho-ahn allowed to address Soo-zee by his hind name. Tonight, however, the familiarity made Soo-zee's crest bristle. He had to remind himself that Little Dinka didn't yet know about Cho-ahn's death.

He waited while Little Dinka scuttled up the tree. When he reached the lookout, Soo-zee did a few push-ups to reassert his dominance. Little Dinka bobbed his head and held up a bag. "Look what I've got, Wanabi."

Soo-zee smelled dinka seeds. "How did you get those? We haven't been paid in over a moon." Little Dinka opened the bag. Soo-zee flicked out his tongue and tasted the air. This long after last year's harvest, the scent of the seeds was faint. Soo-zee couldn't imagine how Little Dinka had gotten them. Soo-zee knew some soldiers would do almost anything for dinka this time of year. Some took on extra patrols. Others picked off another's mites. Some even offered their hindquarters to less dominant soldiers.

Little Dinka bobbed his head to show that the seeds were a gift for Soo-zee. Soo-zee hesitated. There weren't very many seeds in the bag. It would take almost all of them to feel anything. The next full moon was the harvest moon. Seeds would once again become strong and plentiful. He could wait. But it looked as if Littla Dinka couldn't. His tongue and teeth had begun to turn blue, a sure sign of growing addiction.

Soo-zee took a few seeds out of politeness and gave the rest back to Little Dinka. As he chewed, the seeds sent a jolt down his spine. No wonder Little Dinka had been able to buy them. Jacked dinka was cheap. Jacked dinka was strong. Jacked dinka made you do things you later regretted. If Soo-zee had known, he would have declined the offering. But there was nothing to be done for it now.

Little Dinka finished the rest of the seeds. He bobbed his head and presented his hindquarters to Soo-zee. It felt wrong to be coupling on the night of Cho-ahn's execution, but the jacked dinka was insistent. Soo-zee's dewlap puffed up large from his throat. One of his hemipenes everted. He grabbed the back of Little Dinka's neck with his teeth and wrapped his tail under Little Dinka's. He hooked himself into Little Dinka's cloaca, his seminal groove sealing itself as his erectile tissue expanded.

The jacked dinka made their coupling last longer. By the time Soo-zee ejaculated it was fully dark. They sat side by side for a while and listened to the crickets. Their song reminded Soo-zee that he hadn't yet eaten.

"Wanabi, may I ask you a question?"

Soo-zee grunted his assent. He didn't really feel like chirping, not even to tell Little Dinka about Cho-ahn. He wanted to keep his grief private for the moment, even though the others would have to learn about it soon enough. Not that it would matter to Little Dinka. War, like everything else, was just a game to him. The royal army could be around the next copse, but as soon as Soo-zee was gone, Little Dinka would fall asleep, his belief in Night Slayers notwithstanding.

"Have you ever given your hindquarters to anyone?" Little Dinka asked.

"You know I haven't. Why ask?" He could smell his ejaculate in Little Dinka's cloaca, a salty scent that made him think of Cho-ahn.

"I was hoping you might offer them to me someday."

"Is that why you gave me jacked dinka and didn't tell me?"

Little Dinka's crest twitched. He bobbed his head. "Wanabi, no—I would never. I just forgot to tell you."

"You know I would do almost anything for you, Dinkie—but not that."

Little Dinka swallowed his disappointment. "It's not that important, Wanabi." His crest twitched again. "Anyway, you wouldn't be the first."

"The first what?" The jacked dinka made Soo-zee's thoughts slow.

"The first to give me his hindquarters."

Soo-zee's crest bristled. "Who?" Not Cho-ahn, he thought—anyone but Cho-ahn.

Little Dinka looked away. His head bobbed back and forth. "It was Roh-kee," he finally chirped.

Relief made Soo-zee feel light-headed. Or maybe it was just the jacked dinka.

"It was the night Cho-ahn first gave us dinka," Little Dinka chirped. "Cho-ahn took me and I took Roh-kee."

Soo-zee had to fight a momentary urge to slice open Little Dinka's throat. He took several deep breaths and practiced stillness. Wartime liaisons meant nothing. Soldiers carved each other's marks on the forever tree to show dominance and submission, nothing more. They couldn't even eat the fruit of the tree to seal the alliance like they did back home after pair bonding with a female. He and Cho-ahn had tried it. But the forever tree didn't belong here, any more than they did. They had spent the night regurgitating its bitter fruit until there was nothing left inside them.

Soo-zee tried not to think of Cho-ahn with Little Dinka. The idea of Little Dinka with Roh-kee wasn't much better, but at least it hadn't been Roh-koh. Roh-kee might be stupid, but in most ways Roh-koh was worse. When Roh-koh got angry—which was often—he would lash out with his tail at whatever was closest. Usually it was tree trunks, but sometimes it was the burrow walls, or other members of the squad. Once he'd almost put Little Dinka's eye out.

Soo-zee thought back to that night they'd first chewed dinka—*real* dinka, that is, not the three seeds everyone chewed symbolically on Harvest Eve. Those seeds were weak enough for hatchlings and, anyway, they spat those out. The seeds Cho-ahn had given them were *strong*. Soo-zee remembered Little Dinka's nictating membrane partially closing, his hind limbs splaying as the seeds took effect. Cho-ahn did several push-ups and puffed out his dewlap. Soo-zee hadn't really understood what was happening until Cho-ahn sank his teeth into Little Dinka's neck. Soo-zee reacted without thinking. He scuttled forward and bit Cho-ahn's tail—not hard enough to sever it, but hard enough to draw blood. Cho-ahn released Little Dinka and did a series of push-ups. Soo-zee did some push-ups back. They circled each other, tails whipping back and forth. Little Dinka didn't run away, but stood on his hind legs and watched the fight, his pale crest rippling with pleasure.

A sharp series of whistles from Roh-kee stopped them. "Let go, you carrion eaters," he hissed. "No fighting in the burrow." Cho-ahn and Soo-zee released each other. As they sized each other up, the dinka took effect. The burrow began to spin. Soo-zee stumbled to a corner and closed his eyes. He saw his father, who had died while Soo-zee was a hatchling. He conversed with the Iridescent Spirit. He saw Cho-ahn, Little Dinka and Roh-kee in a three-stack, their tails entwined in a beautiful braid.

Soo-zee looked at Little Dinka. "Then it wasn't a vision I had that night. You… Cho-ahn…"

Little Dinka bobbed his head. "Don't be jealous, Wanabi. Your mark is the only one carved with mine on the forever tree and mine the only one with yours."

"What do you mean? Cho-ahn and I carved our marks there moons ago."

Little Dinka's crest rippled with annoyance. "Well mine is the only mark there with yours now."

"Dinkie, what have you done?" A powerful emotion shook Soo-zee's crest. "I have to return to camp." He scuttled down the tree. At the bottom he looked back up and waited for Little Dinka to bob a farewell, but the scout was cleaning his cloaca with his tongue. After a while Soo-zee got tired of waiting and trudged back to camp to tell the others the bad news, resisting the urge to make a detour to the forever tree. Marks on a tree were just symbols, he told himself—nothing more. Love and hate were things you carried inside yourself. No one could take them from you unless you let them.

2

Two mornings later, there was a blue at training. "Pay attention, fecal brains," Bah-kah chirped. "This is your new code breaker."

"Your new code breaker," Goo-nah repeated his nose a scale behind Bah-kah's hindquarters.

Soo-zee examined the blue. He was barely more than a hatchling with big dark eyes. He was smaller even than Little Dinka.

The squad flicked their tails in disapproval. "Why do we even need a code breaker?" Little Dinka asked.

"Because," Bah-kah hissed, "you feces-smeared carrion-eaters are not a complete squad without a code breaker. Until you are a complete squad, Rebel Command cannot use you in combat. If you cannot be used in combat, *I* cannot get promoted." *Thwack.* "*I* will not receive a bonus." *Thwack.* "*I* will not be happy." Goo-nah smacked Roh-koh with the back of his claw. Roh-koh glared at the new recruit.

"Your breaker's name is Jee-ahn Inari. See that you make him welcome. Or you can all go back to your home burrows. Oh, wait... I forgot—you can't."

Goo-nah's crest rippled with amusement. No burrow could take in a rebel soldier, not even his own. His Grace's spies were everywhere. A burrow suspected of so much as giving a rebel food would be destroyed, not even the hatchlings spared. The Rohs had found that out when they tried to desert and the royal army wiped out their burrow. By sheer luck, the brothers had been away looking for dinka when it happened. A tenday after leaving, they had come crawling back, half-starved. Bobbing their heads in submission, they'd begged Bah-kah to take them back. Bah-kah had hissed for more than a tenclick, whipping his tail back and forth while Goo-nah struck them. But his orange crest had barely moved, proving to Soo-zee that the display of anger was all for show. Only Little Dinka had been afraid. His silvered crest had trembled and it had taken a clawful of dinka to calm him down.

"Trainee Jee-ahn," Bah-kah chirped. "You are now a provisional member of this squad. Work hard and you will be promoted to Novice. Fail and the entire squad will feel my wrath." Goo-nah whipped his tail around and smacked Soo-zee. Soo-zee kept his crest neutral and looked at the ground.

Jee-ahn bobbed his head in submission and fell

into line next to Little Dinka. Up close, Soo-zee could see that his scales would be a deep indigo once he shed. Healthy blues were a rarity, but Jee-ahn had no visible mites. Even this close to shedding, he was beautiful. Roh-kee's throat pulsed briefly, a fact not lost on Little Dinka, whose crest bristled with resentment. Soo-zee felt one of his own hemipenes start to evert. There would be a fight over Jee-ahn somewhere down the line and Soo-zee only hoped it wouldn't come after he'd eaten jacked dinka. He might get confused and stake his hindquarters; he might get confused and lose. He had no intention of letting the Rohs or anyone else dominate *him*.

As soon as they started drilling, it became apparent that Jee-ahn knew nothing about fighting, not even the right way to hold a stick. He learned quickly, but it wasn't enough for the Rohs.

"Everyone knows that blues are sneaky," Roh-kee chirped to the others when they took a basking break. "While you're out hunting, they'll snatch your mate right out of your nest." Jee-ahn was neck-deep in the river, drowning any mites he might have picked up during practice. He either didn't hear Roh-kee or pretended not to.

"You don't have a mate," Soo-zee pointed out. "None of us do."

Roh-kee did a push-up.

"I don't like him," Roh-koh hissed. He struck a nearby bush with his tail. Twigs and leaves went flying.

"It could be worse," Roh-kee chirped. "He could be green, like Porter." Greens were considered the lowest of the low, fit only for menial labor. They didn't even have names so far as the camp was concerned – just occupations.

"Porter is totally devoted to us," Soo-zee chirped. "Not that we've done anything to deserve it."

Jee-ahn crawled out of the river. In the sun his wet scales appeared almost purple.

"Maybe we should give him a chance," Roh-kee chirped with another brief pulsing of his throat. Soo-zee wondered what it would be like to couple with a blue. He'd heard they had especially sharp claws.

That night, Soo-zee couldn't sleep. He felt agitated; he felt aroused. He missed Cho-ahn. He rubbed his hemipenes against the ground and chirped to Little Dinka, but there was no answer and the scout's nest was empty. Roh-koh and Roh-kee were asleep in their shared nest. Jee-ahn was tossing and turning in his. Soo-zee went out to the drill yard to look for Little Dinka. The moon was nearly full. Soon it would be time for the harvest. If Bah-kah actually gave them their back pay, as promised, Soo-zee would be able to buy Little Dinka fresh seeds.

A sound at the edge of the yard caught Soo-zee's attention. He flattened himself and scuttled forward. Just inside the bushes that lined the yard, Goo-nah lay next to Little Dinka. His hindquarters were pressed under Little Dinka's tail. Soo-zee watched for a while, aroused and angry in equal measure.

He returned to the burrow and watched Jee-ahn tossing in his nest. He tapped him awake and did several rapid push-ups. Jee-ahn just looked at him with those dark, shiny eyes. His crest never even quivered. Soo-zee pumped up his dewlap. Still Jee-ahn did not offer his hindquarters. Soo-zee decided not to force the issue. If Jee-ahn deserted, there was no telling what Bah-kah might do.

Soo-zee returned to his nest and waited for Little Dinka to return, but the scout did not appear. He rubbed his hemipenes against the ground until he ejaculated. After a while, he drifted off to sleep.

For the next quarter moon, they drilled harder than ever. Soo-zee thought of Cho-ahn less and less often and was so tired in the evenings that he didn't even care that Little Dinka was seldom in his nest at lights out.

One night, though, he heard noises in the entryway and got up to see what it was about. He found Little Dinka, Bah-kah and Goo-nah with their heads together, their crests bristling with excitement.

"What's going on?" Soo-zee asked.

"We have decided to promote Jee-ahn from Trainee to Novice," Bah-kah chirped. "Just before we shed our old skins, we will invite Rebel Command to evaluate the squad. It's all you have sacrificed for, Soo-zee Wanabi. You will be a full-fledged rebel soldier."

"I don't think he's ready," Soo-zee chirped. He wondered why he hadn't been invited to this meeting, why Roh-koh and Roh-kee, the senior members of the squad, had not been asked.

"He just needs to relax," Bah-kah chirped. Goo-nah and Little Dinka rippled their crests. Soo-zee didn't see what was so funny.

"Return to your nest, Soo-zee Wanabi," Goo-nah chirped. "This doesn't concern you."

Soo-zee bobbed his head and went back to his nest, waiting for Little Dinka to come tell him what was going on. But he must have fallen asleep, for the next thing he knew he was starting awake from a nightmare about a Slayer. He could still feel the Slayer's claws on his shoulder, taste the Slayer's scent on his tongue.

Little Dinka was asleep. Soo-zee shook him awake. Little Dinka hissed at him with blue-tinged teeth. "Go away."

"Get up," Soo-zee hissed.

Little Dinka tried to lash Soo-zee with his tail but missed. Soo-zee noticed mites on the underside of Little Dinka's neck and started to pick them off, but the scout slapped his claws away. "I can take care of myself."

Soo-zee did a push-up and pulled him to his feet. "Then do it."

Little Dinka rocked unsteadily and fell to all fours. "I'm fine, Wanabi. I don't need you to look after me." He turned to his water bowl and looked at his reflection. Soo-zee left him in the burrow. Little Dinka's grooming could take tenclicks.

Bah-kah and Goo-nah let Little Dinka's tardiness slide. But they were merciless when anyone in the squad made a mistake. Every one of them went to sleep that night with torn skin and bruises. By Harvest Moon Eve, they looked like they'd been through a battle. Soo-zee was sad they would be shedding their scars with their old skins. They'd earned those scars through hard work and sacrifice. But soon they'd be earning real battle scars, some of which might last many sheddings.

Bah-kah dismissed them early and Porter built a fire in the drill yard. When they'd all gathered round, Goo-nah gave them a present—the last of the year's old dinka. "This dinka represents you," he chirped. "It is weak now, but tomorrow it will be strong. Let us celebrate your coming strength by chewing the old year out together."

He offered the bag to the Rohs first. Roh-kee took an extra-large clawful, enough to make him stupider and then some. Soo-zee was next. He took a small clawful, enough for a pleasant sensation, but not so much that he couldn't couple if Little Dinka was willing. Little Dinka took a clawful, too. Then he took a clawful more. Soo-zee's hemepenes throbbed, even as he worried about how much Little Dinka was chewing.

Goo-nah held the bag out to Jee-ahn. The breaker declined.

"Have some," Goo-nah insisted. "It's tradition."

"I can't break code on dinka," Jee-ahn chirped.

"It's end-of-year seeds. They aren't very strong. Mothers give them to their hatchlings."

"Nevertheless, I respectfully decline, Goo-nah Kisasu." Jee-ahn chirped, with a bob of his head.

"As you wish, Jee-ahn Inari." Goo-nah offered the sack to Soo-zee, who accepted with a bob of his head. Halfway through chewing, he realized he could no longer feel his hind legs. *Not strong, my hindquarters*, he thought. The dinka had been jacked. He turned to take Goo-nah to task, but Goo-nah was already halfway across the yard with Roh-kee and Little Dinka. Roh-koh was bashing one of Porter's logs. His tail leaked green blood everywhere, but he looked as if he didn't even feel it.

Soo-zee wondered what he had done to push Little Dinka away. He saw Jee-ahn looking at him. It's you, Soo-zee thought. All this started the day you joined us. He tried to flick his tail in annoyance, but it wouldn't respond. Instead he hissed; but the code breaker was gone. Soo-zee staggered back toward the burrow. Halfway there, he fell unconscious.

He woke in his nest with no idea how he'd gotten there. The rest of the squad was in their nests as well, save for Jee-ahn. Soo-zee closed his eyes and tried to go back to sleep, but he couldn't stop thinking about Little Dinka. Little Dinka and Cho-ahn… Little Dinka and Goo-nah… Little Dinka and everyone but him. They had a free day in honor of the harvest, the first without drills since the last harvest moon. If he didn't stop thinking about Cho-ahn and Little Dinka he would soon go as mad as the Rohs thought His Grace was. Maybe Goo-nah had some leftover seeds. Just a few jacked seeds would keep him from thinking. Just a few wouldn't hurt.

He got out of his nest and watched Little Dinka sleep. His lips had taken on a deeper shade of blue. He looked at Jee-ahn's empty nest and tried to imagine what the breaker would look like after eating dinka. A blue lizard with a blue tongue and teeth. Now that would be something.

Little Dinka opened his eyes. He flicked out his tongue in a sleepy greeting. "Come into my nest, Wanabi," he chirped.

Soo-zee hesitated. Little Dinka flicked his tongue again. "Not to couple—to snuggle," he chirped. "Come."

Even as he thought of reasons to refuse, his hindquarters propelled him forward. The nest smelled of dinka and of salt that wasn't his. Little Dinka flicked his tongue toward Soo-zee's cloaca. "Tonight, after the campfire, my hindquarters are yours and yours alone."

Soo-zee's dewlap puffed up despite his best efforts to control it. This time, however, when he closed his eyes, no unwanted visions troubled his sleep.

3

The trees surrounding the camp were dark behind the Harvest Eve fire. Soo-zee felt sure His Grace's armies must be marching to destroy them despite the holiday truce, perhaps with the sharpened sticks of metal they called "blades." Jee-ahn had been monitoring the radio for signs of treachery, but there had been none. His Grace had even granted amnesty to a clawful of condemned prisoners, though his own father's burrow brother wasn't one of them. He was to be sacrificed on Burrow Town's holiday fire along with the traditional crickets.

Porter threw another branch on the fire and Goo-nah passed a jug of forever berry wine. It was strong and sweet, just like the forever berries Soo-zee had known as a hatchling. Wherever Goo-nah was buying his contraband, it was good. They each sacrificed a cricket for a prosperous year, along with an extra one for the Iridescent Spirit. Afterward, Little Dinka entertained them with scary stories about Night Slayer raids on unwary Harvest celebrants.

"You never see them coming," he chirped. "They're dark as night teeth to tail. No weapons but their claws. And they eat hatchlings like Roh-kee eats dinka." Everyone's crest rippled.

"Ah, yes—dinka," Goo-nah chirped. He produced a bag and offered it to Bah-kah. "Fresh from today's harvest."

"Dinka is not allowed in camp," Bah-kah replied. His crest rippled with amusement. He took a clawful and put it in his mouth. Goo-noh took some next, then passed the bag to Roh-koh. Around the circle the bag went, everyone taking some and chewing. When the bag got to Jee-ahn, however, he gave it to Porter instead.

Goo-nah snatched the bag from Porter's claws. "No dinka for greens. But blues... now that's another story."

"I don't want any," Jee-ahn chirped with a head bob.

Bah-kah got up and walked over to Jee-ahn. He did several push-ups. "You will partake with your squad."

"Respectfully, Bah-kah Takebi... I will not." Jee-ahn bobbed his head.

"You will," Bah-kah hissed. His tail whipped around so fast the yellow streak looked like fire. It sliced the skin above Jee-ahn's eye. Bah-kah's dewlap pulsed coral. Green blood dripped into Jee-ahn's eye. Bah-kah raised his claws again. The breaker turned and scuttled toward the bushes.

"Get him," Bah-kah hissed. The Rohs gave chase. They caught him and dragged him back to the fire, ignoring the lashings of his sharp tail.

"Porter, come here," Bah-kah ordered. Porter came forward and bobbed his head.

"Hit him," Bah-kah hissed.

Porter bobbed his head up and down. "Let him go," he chirped.

"I will banish you from this camp, you fecal-stained worm." Bah-kah did a series of furious push-ups. "Hit him." Porter bobbed his head but did not obey. Bah-kah lashed his tail and sliced Porter's crest. Porter stood his ground.

"Roh-kee, you hit him," Bah-kah chirped. Roh-kee released his hold on Jee-ahn's neck and raised a claw.

"No," Porter chirped. Jee-ahn's crest shook with fear.

"Shut up," Roh-kee hissed. He slapped Porter's face with the back of his claw.

"You hit like a female," Bah-kah chirped. "A warrior hits like this." He backclawed Jee-ahn's jaw. There was a loud crack and Jee-ahn spat out a tooth. His mouth drooled blood and saliva. Roh-kee raised his claw.

"Please…" Jee-ahn chirped, looking at Roh-kee with eyes as big as the moon. Roh-kee hesitated.

Bah-kah whipped his tail. A chunk of Roh-kee's skin went flying. Roh-kee smashed his claws against Jee-ahn's jaw.

"Open his mouth," Bah-kah hissed.

Porter placed himself between Bah-kah and Jee-ahn. "Bah-kah Takebi, stop this at once, or I will report you to Rebel Command."

"Do it and I will denounce your burrow to His Disgrace. Your females and your puke-colored hatchlings will die. Don't think I won't do it, you fecal-smeared fly eater. Now move or kiss their memories goodbye." Porter reluctantly stood aside.

"Bah-kah, haven't we had our fun?" Goo-nah's head bobbed so fast Soo-zee could barely see it move. A chunk of his crest, too, went flying.

"Little Dinka, come here," Bah-kah ordered.

Soo-zee looked at Little Dinka and shook his head. Little Dinka's eyes appeared dull and shot through with green, an effect of too much dinka. Soo-zee wanted to hiss at him to sit down. But he didn't. He told himself it was because he was scared of Bah-kah. He told himself it was because of the dinka.

Little Dinka stood in front of Jee-ahn. Bah-kah did a push-up. "Take some dinka. Chew, but don't swallow." With a head bob, Little Dinka obeyed.

"Goo-nah, open his mouth," Bah-kah chirped. Goo-nah started to pry open Jee-ahn's jaws.

The breaker snapped them shut.

"Help me," Goo-nah grunted to Soo-zee. Soo-zee stayed where he was. He waited for the blow, but none came. Little Dinka was helping Goo-nah force open Jee-ahn's mouth. It was no easy task. Blues had the bite strength of an iguana. But even a blue could not hold out forever. Eventually, Jee-ahn's jaws parted. Little Dinka spat the chewed up seeds into his mouth. Jee-ahn thrashed and tried to spit them out. But Little Dinka and Goo-nah held his mouth shut.

"Swallow," Goo-nah hissed.

Jee-ahn rippled his crest in defiance. Goo-nah hit him and covered his nose.

A click passed... two... three. Suddenly Jee-ahn whipped his tail. It sliced open Roh-koh's snout. Roh-koh shrieked and let go. Jee-ahn's hind quarters thrashed.

"Keep him down," Bah-kah hissed. Roh-koh bashed Jee-ahn with his tail and sat on him. Jee-ahn stopped moving. Another several clicks passed. The breaker didn't move at all. Soo-zee thought they might have killed him.

Finally, Jee-ahn's tail twitched and he swallowed. Goo-nah uncovered his nose. The breaker gasped for air and swiveled his eyes, looking for an escape route. His eyes met Soo-zee's and silently pleaded for help.

Soo-zee looked away. By the time he dared look back, the dinka had begun take effect. Jee-ahn's hind legs splayed. The nictating membrane over his eyes closed. If Soo-zee was going to do something, it had to be now.

He stood. He looked at Jee-ahn's bloody face. He looked at Bah-kah. He sat back down.

"Let him go," Bah-kah chirped. "Sit. Watch. Learn."

The others returned to their places. Bah-kah did a series of push-ups. His dewlap began to swell. "You do not contradict me," he hissed.

Jee-ahn pushed himself to his feet. His legs failed and he fell to the ground. Bah-kah swiped a claw at his neck. A gaping wound dripped blood.

"I am your commander." Bah-kah swiped again. His claws carved slices in Jee-ahn's chest, revealing fresh violet beneath the old, white skin. "I am your only deity." He whipped his tail and caught Jee-ahn on the jaw. Another wound sprouted green. He walked in a circle around Jee-ahn, his dewlap large and coral.

"Please," Jee-ahn chirped. He tried to scuttle away but his legs refused to obey his brain's command.

"Beg," Bah-kah hissed. He was behind Jee-ahn now, watching the breaker's crest twitch.

Jee-ahn bobbed his head. "Please, Bah-kah Takebi… I beg you."

"Well, now how can I deny you when you beg so sweetly?" Bah-kah's dewlap bulged larger still. It looked to Soo-zee as if it would burst. With a grunt the commander lunged forward and sank his teeth into

Jee-ahn's neck. The breaker's claws scrabbled as he tried to escape. Bah-kah held on tightly. Ever so slowly, he wrapped his tail under Jee-ahn's. Jee-ahn's hind feet slowly rose into the air.

The two lay entwined for a tenclick. Soo-zee wanted to make it stop, but a sick fascination made him watch, especially as Bah-kah kept rotating his eyes to see if they were looking. Finally he unhooked himself and removed his tail from Jee-ahn's hindquarters. The breaker scuttled away. Bah-kah stood and faced the others, his hemipenis still everted. While they watched, he flicked out his tongue and cleaned it. No one dared look away. They had no thought to spare for Jee-ahn as he dragged his battered body toward the burrow.

Soo-zee liked to think he would have done something had Bah-kah not been watching them. But in truth, he was just relieved that it hadn't been him.

The next morning, when Soo-zee awoke, Jee-ahn's nest was empty. The rest of the squad was already in the yard.

"Where's Jee-ahn?" Soo-zee asked. The Rohs and Little Dinka grunted. Their eyes were shot through with green. "Shouldn't we go look for him? We have to do something."

"What can we do?" Roh-koh chirped. "Report him to Rebel Command? We're not even officially part of the company yet. All they'll do is punish us for doing dinka. They might even banish us."

"At least let's confer with Goo-nah, maybe he can—" Soo zee stopped short. Jee-ahn had appeared at the side of the yard. The blue picked up his stick from the rack and took his usual place. Soo-zee looked at the others. They should say something, he thought. He started forward. A claw clamped down on his shoulder.

"Let it go," Little Dinka chirped. "We shouldn't have let it happen. But we did. Reminding him will only make it worse."

Jee-ahn had started going through the pre-drill. Perhaps Little Dinka was right. Maybe the best thing was to pretend last night had never happened.

"We're late," Roh-koh chirped. "If Bah-kah comes out now we're all in for a beating." They got their sticks from the racks, keeping their distance from Jee-ahn without realizing it. The breaker kept on drilling, never once looking up.

They were relieved of their uncertainty by the arrival of Goo-nah from the officer's burrow. Thankfully, Bah-kah wasn't with him.

"Let's run through drill 37," Goo-nah chirped. He worked them hard, without a break. They had no time for conversation. After training, Soo-zee hung back, intending to ask Jee-ahn if there was anything he could do for him. But Little Dinka flicked his tongue at Soo-zee's cloaca and beckoned him to the

side of the yard. Soo-zee's dewlap puffed up and he
followed.

When they reached the bushes, Soo-zee glanced
back over his shoulder. Jee-ahn was staring at them,
his black eyes impossible to read.

4

Soo-zee looked for an opportunity to chirp with Jee-ahn, but it never seemed to be the right time. There was always someone else there, some drill to get through, some chore to do. With every day that passed, broaching the subject became more awkward. How to explain why he hadn't done anything to stop it, even if he could have... but of course he couldn't, how could he, how could they? They were too young, they were too scared, there were only five of them, there was the dinka, and really, when you thought about it, wasn't it Jee-ahn's own fault? All he'd had to do was be one of them, just for a night. All he'd had to do was chew some dinka. Whenever Jee-ahn looked at him, Soo-zee felt a deep sense of shame. He started making excuses to avoid the breaker. If Jee-ahn came into the room, Soo-zee found something that needed doing elsewhere. When he had watch with Jee-ahn, he heard lots of suspicious noises in the undergrowth he needed to check.

No matter how early Soo-zee arrived at the drill yard, Jee-ahn was already there practicing. When they left in the evening, he stayed behind. The sight of him doing the same drills over and over began to put Soo-zee into a bad temper. Part of it was just the usual pre-shedding irritability. But it was also something more, a growing sense that Jee-ahn's behavior was Soo-zee's fault. If he'd been able, he would have avoided the breaker completely. But Rebel Command had finally agreed to give them a try-out. That meant more time in the yard, more time working together closely. Soo-zee would not give up all he had worked for just because one weak blue couldn't stand up for himself. Though he had to admit, that might not be true any longer. The hours of extra drilling had improved Jee-ahn's fighting to the point where he was better now than Little Dinka, much to the latter's dismay. Little Dinka snapped at Jee-ahn constantly, finding fault with everything he did. He was spending more nights away from his nest, too, and his teeth had turned a deeper blue, worn down as much from scrubbing them with a twig in a futile effort to keep them white as from chewing dinka.

Soo-zee began to worry about Little Dinka in earnest. His fears kept him from sleeping. The only thing that helped was dinka, but Soo-zee was afraid of becoming reliant on it. On his worst nights he would walk around the perimeter and try not to think. But sometimes he would see Little Dinka scuttling away from the officer's burrow and all his doubts would creep back in.

The night before the try-out, three officers from Rebel Command arrived and were taken to the officers' burrow. After training, the squad basked in the river and tried to make themselves presentable— not an easy task with peeling white skin nearly ready for shedding. The Rohs groomed each other, while Soo-zee and Little Dinka checked each other for mites. Only Jee-ahn stood alone, licking his scales over and over, even though they were already as pristine as old skin could be. He had almost completely healed from Bah-kah's beating, save for a few bright blue patches where Bah-kah had slashed away his old skin. Elsewhere, he was as pale as Little Dinka's crest. Against the sand at the river's edge he was almost invisible. If it hadn't been for those big accusing eyes, Soo-zee could have pretended he didn't exist.

That night Soo-zee was too excited to sleep. He gave up and decided to walk the perimeter. On his way out, he was relieved to see that Little Dinka was still in his nest. Roh-kee, however, was gone from his.

Soo-zee started his circuit. As he approached the officer's burrow, something knocked him on his side. *A Slayer!* he thought, his heart in his throat. But it was only Roh-kee.

"Look what I've got," Roh-kee chirped. He held up a sack of dinka.

"Where'd you get that?" Soo-zee asked. They still hadn't been given their back pay. Whenever they asked, Bah-kah's dewlap puffed up threateningly and Goo-nah told them it was being held up by Rebel Command.

"One of the command officer's packs," Roh-kee chirped.

"You can't!" Soo-zee squeaked. "What happens when he finds out?"

"Who cares? Think of this as our back pay. Here… have some—it's totally pure, the real deal." He opened the sack and scooped a clawful of seeds into his mouth. His crest shook with pleasure.

Soo-zee took some and chewed. Real dinka would help him sleep. "Are you going to share it with the others?"

"We don't have to if you don't want to," Roh-kee chirped. He did a few pushups and puffed out his dewlap. "You lose, you pick my mites. You win, you can have my hindquarters."

Soo-zee didn't want Roh-kee's hindquarters. But he wanted a target for his anger. He lunged at Roh-kee and bared his teeth. Roh-kee raised his claws.

They fought for almost three tenclicks, until their jaws were locked on each other's in a deadly kiss, their legs trembling with the effort. In the end, Roh-kee submitted. Soo-zee's dewlap puffed large in triumph and when Roh-kee presented his hindquarters, it was all Soo-zee could do to hold back until they made it into the bushes beside the river. When he'd had his fill of both the dinka and Roh-kee, Soo-zee returned to the burrow, leaving Roh-kee behind to wash.

He was awakened by Jee-ahn shaking his shoulder. "Time to wake up, Soo-zee Wanabi. Big day. You're running late." Soo-zee looked around. The other nests were empty. If Little Dinka was already awake, he must be very late, indeed. He hurried to the yard.

Roh-koh and Little Dinka were pacing back and forth, their crests twitching in agitation.

"Have you seen my brother?" Roh-koh asked. "He wasn't in the nest when I woke up."

"I haven't seen him since last night," Soo-zee answered, almost truthfully. "Maybe he went to the officers' burrow to get Goo-nah."

But Goo-nah was already coming toward them, accompanied by Bah-kah and the officers from Rebel Command. One of the junior officers was hissing at the other, his crest bristling with anger. Bah-kah and Goo-nah kept bobbing their heads in submission.

"Move your hindquarters," Soo-zee hissed. "The officers don't look happy." The others took their places.

Bah-kah's crest bristled when he saw that Roh-kee wasn't there.

"Bah-kah Takebi, you told us your squad was ready." The senior officer's crest twitched stiffly.

"Roh-koh Onono," Bah-kah chirped. "Where is Roh-kee Kazeyo?"

"He was up early this morning. Perhaps his skin was shedding early."

"Go check by the river," Bah-kah commanded. "Little Dinka, check the perimeter. Jee-ahn, return to the burrow and see if there is any sign of where he might have gone. Soo-zee, you and Goo-nah search the forest." His head bobbed furiously.

Soo-zee headed for the forever tree, resisting the urge to run toward the river. Maybe Roh-kee had decided to carve his and Soo-zee's marks. He had already carved his and Little Dinka's on one branch, and his and Roh-koh's on another. It would be just like him to carve Soo-zee's mark after giving him his hindquarters.

But Roh-kee wasn't at the forever tree and Soo-zee didn't see his and Roh-kee's marks on it. Nor did he see the branch where he'd carved his and Cho-ahn's marks. True to Little Dinka's word, it was gone. The tree's fruits had ripened with the harvest moon and now hung heavy, their bitter juices dripping onto the ground. Beyond the tree the forest loomed dark and menacing. He imagined an army of Night Slayers high in the branches, their darkened scales invisible against the canopy. Suddenly he didn't want to find Roh-kee.

A wail came from the direction of the river and grew in volume. Soo-zee turned and ran toward it, as fast as he'd ever run. The keening was coming from Roh-koh. Roh-kee lay unmoving in his arms, his tongue lolling dry and blue from his gaping mouth.

"What happened?" Soo-zee asked.

"Dinka!" Bah-kah hissed.

"We will report this to Command," the senior officer chirped. "Dinka has no place in the rebel army."

"I assure you," Bah-kah chirped, his head bobbing more rapidly than ever, "my squads do not chew dinka. We will investigate this and determine how it happened."

"See that you do, Bah-kah Takebi. We will return in one moon cycle. If the squad is not complete by then, you will be demoted and the camp assigned to another commander. In the meantime, we are sorry for your loss."

As they took their leave, one of the junior officers turned and eyed the squad. Soo-zee did his best to look innocent.

"Where are we going to get another soldier before the next moon?" Goo-nah asked.

"How can you think about that when Roh-kee has just died?" Soo-zee hissed.

"We are at war," Bah-kah chirped. "We bury our dead and we mourn them, but we fight on. We need someone with experience to replace Roh-kee and we need him now. Do any of you know of anyone who would be willing to join us?"

The squad shifted uneasily. No one wanted to put his burrow at risk.

Jee-ahn's crest twitched nervously. "I know someone," he chirped at last. "Shi-ahn Hatari—from my burrow. His grandfather was Shi-ahn Hasuri, who died at the Long Burrows Siege."

"I know of Shi-ahn Hasuri," Bah-kah chirped. "If he was from your burrow, I am surprised His Disgrace has not destroyed it. Goo-nah, have Porter go to Jee-ahn's burrow and request young Shi-ahn's enlistment." That was another good thing about letting greens into the army as far as Soo-zee was concerned. No one noticed them. They could beg from burrow to burrow without attracting attention.

After Goo-nah left, they prepared Roh-kee's body for cremation. They cleaned the feces from his cloaca and scrubbed his teeth with a twig until they were almost white. Porter built a pyre of duckwood logs, which would burn hot enough to carry Roh-kee's spirit to the World between Worlds. There he would stand watch with the Iridescent Spirit for a full moon cycle before joining his ancestors in the Forever World. Or at least that was what tradition held. Soo-zee didn't believe in the Forever World or the Iridescent Spirit. They were just stories for gullible hatchlings, no different than Night Slayers or any other tale.

When the ceremony was over, they scattered Roh-kee's ashes around the base of the forever tree. Soo-zee wondered whether there was supposed to be dinka in the Forever World. He wasn't sure if that would be a good thing or not.

5

They worked as hard as grief would allow. But Roh-koh kept breaking off in the middle of a drill to stare toward the river with drooping crest. At other times, he would storm off to the forever tree, lashing it over and over until both his tail and the bark were raw and covered in bitter goo. Sometimes he would strike one of his squad mates, usually Jee-ahn or Little Dinka. "You don't deserve to be here," he would hiss. "You weren't fit to pick his mites."

He couldn't say the same about Shi-ahn Hatari, the new recruit, though. Shi-ahn was good. He was the same dark blue as Jee-ahn, but bigger, stronger and faster. He could also break code tolerably well, if not as fast as Jee-ahn. He and Jee-ahn spent all their spare time together, inventing ciphers with which to stump each other. Little Dinka was leaving the nest nearly every night after lights out now, returning before dawn smelling of Goo-nah and dinka. He spent more and more time scrubbing his teeth on waking, arriving so late to training that Bah-kah finally ordered Goo-nah to search their nests for dinka. Goo-nah, of course, found nothing. Meanwhile, Roh-koh was stripping the bark from half the forest with his tail. Soo-zee had never felt more alone.

One night, Jee-ahn returned from listening to His Grace's address and announced that the royal army had seized the burrow where the rebels kept most of their food stores. There had been a heavily coded message as well, one neither Jee-ahn nor Shi-ahn could break. All he could tell the squad was that it contained the code for "slayer." The news had everyone on edge, even Soo-zee.

The next day Bah-kah told them that Command had put the camp on half-rations. By the following week they had been cut in half yet again. Even with the loss of appetite that preceded shedding, it was hard to drill on quarter rations. It was particularly difficult for the blues, who burned fuel at a faster rate than the others. Porter tried giving Jee-ahn and Shi-ahn his rations, but the two wouldn't take them. Bah-kah set out for Command to beg for more food, taking Porter with him and leaving the camp in Goo-nah's care. Two days later, however, Goo-nah announced that he and Little Dinka were leaving to forage. The others were on their own.

The rest of them bickered over whether to conserve their energy or drill without Little Dinka. The point became moot when three days passed and neither the weekly food delivery nor Goo-nah and Little Dinka had returned.

They decided to forage, too, but found nothing more than a dead mouse. Hungry as they were, the blues refused to eat it. But though the decomposing meat turned Soo-zee's stomach, he ate his share when Roh-koh offered it. It tasted worse coming up than it had going down.

The next morning only Roh-koh had enough energy to forage. Thankfully, Goo-nah and Little Dinka returned before sunset, carrying a pitifully small bag of crickets, which the squad shared, except for a few saved for Roh-koh, who was still out foraging. Goo-nah and Little Dinka ate their meal with teeth stained dark blue, and Soo-zee wondered how they had been able to pay for both dinka and crickets. Little Dinka's eyes were dull, and he gave off a pungent odor quite different from his usual smell. Soo-zee suspected they had traded his hindquarters for the food and drugs. He was too tired and hungry to care. He only wished they had gotten more crickets and less dinka.

Roh-koh had not returned by lights out. The crickets wouldn't keep for long, so they divided Roh-koh's share and ate them. Soo-zee hoped that wherever he was, Roh-koh had managed to find food.

The next morning, when they went to get fresh water from the river, they found Roh-koh's body. He had drowned himself during the night. Clutched in his claw was the branch from the forever tree containing his and Roh-kee's marks.

They burned Roh-koh's body and went to the forever tree to spread his ashes on top of Roh-kee's. Some of the fruit had fallen and lay rotting on the ground. They cleared it away as best they could, but it left behind a sticky residue that was impossible to remove. Roh-koh's ashes stuck to it when they spread them.

Afterward, they went back to the burrow and avoided each other's eyes. There was no point in drilling without food since Rebel Command would never take them now. They waited listlessly for several more days, waiting to be reassigned or to starve. As the days wore on and their strength waned, the latter seemed more likely.

Bah-kah finally returned from headquarters empty handed. Rather than being sad at Roh-koh's death, he was angry that Goo-nah hadn't found a replacement.

"Get us another soldier," he hissed. "Command is letting us keep the squad. I don't care if you have to offer your hindquarters to potential recruits. I'm sure there's a big, mean, green somewhere that would love to take them."

Bah-kah must really be desperate, Soo-zee thought, if he was willing to accept a green into the squad. Or maybe he had gone mad. Between the hunger and their imminent shedding, they were all acting a little strange. Soo-zee was so hungry he was ready to try the fruit of the forever tree again.

Soo-zee's sleep grew worse than ever. A few nights after Roh-koh's funeral, while he lay awake trying not to think about Cho-ahn or food, Goo-nah sneaked into the burrow. He pleaded with Little Dinka to run away with him at first light. Soo-zee crawled out of his nest and scuttled over to Jee-ahn's. He put his claws over Jee-ahn's mouth but the breaker was already awake.

Jee-ahn gestured to Soo-zee to climb into his nest. Soo-zee did so. It was a tight fit. "Lie here and pretend to sleep," Jee-ahn chirped softly. "Don't let Goo-nah leave before I get back." He disappeared without a sound. Soo-zee closed his eyes and listened to Goo-nah and Little Dinka. He hoped he wouldn't have to confront Goo-nah. If Little Dinka saw him in Jee-ahn's nest, he would assume he and the breaker had coupled. It might make him run off with Goo-nah. Or it might not, which in some ways would be worse. He forced himself to lie still. Jee-ahn's nest smelled different than his or Little Dinka's. He flicked out his tongue. The air tasted crisp, like the forest after a rainstorm. He wondered if that was a blue thing. Despite the circumstances, Soo-zee found himself becoming aroused. He concentrated on what Goo-nah was chirping. Something about a burrow that might be willing to take them in—something about dinka.

He almost shrieked as Jee-ahn climbed back into the nest. Damn the Iridescent Spirit if he wasn't silent as a Slayer.

Jee-ahn opened his claws and showed Soo-zee a bag of dinka. He pointed to Soo-zee, then to Little Dinka. Soo-zee understood. It was up to him to keep Little Dinka from leaving. They waited, crammed together in the tiny nest. With Jee-ahn there, the rainstorm smell was stronger. Soo-zee's hemipenes swelled. To distract himself, he thought about Goonah's switch; he thought about executions; he thought about Slayers. Nothing seemed to work.

At last, Goo-nah left. Soo-zee climbed out of Jee-ahn's nest, checking to see if Little Dinka was looking. But he was facing the other way, deep in thought. Soo-zee climbed into his nest and opened the bag. Each of them chewed a clawful.

"I'm going to leave with Goo-nah in the morning," Little Dinka chirped tiredly. "There's nothing for me here." Soo-zee felt as if someone had lashed his entrails. He tried to imagine life without Little Dinka. The thought made his crest tremble. The dinka finally kicked in. Soo-zee took a deep breath and forced himself to do the unthinkable.

He bobbed his head and offered Little Dinka his hindquarters.

6

After that, it became a contest between Goo-nah and Soo-zee to see who could get Little Dinka more seeds. Goo-nah seemed to have an endless supply. Their back pay had still not come through, and to get seeds of his own, Soo-zee had to offer his hindquarters to an orange officer with a missing tail. He no longer cared. The officer's dinka was purer than Goo-nah's and Little Dinka liked it better. Soo-zee liked it, too. He didn't even protest when the officer took him to the forever tree to carve their marks; though his crest bristled when he saw that someone had already carved Little Dinka's with Goo-nah's. And when the officer insisted on coupling in the open next to the forever tree so that anyone could see, Soo-zee just chewed some extra dinka and pretended it was Little Dinka. Unfortunately, the officer liked to bite hard. Soo-zee stared into the distance as the officer sank his jaws into Soo-zee's neck. A pale crest twitched beneath the moonlight. Good. Little Dinka was watching. Maybe he'd be jealous.

The orange officer pressed his tailless hindquarters against Soo-zee's. He hooked his hemipenis into Soo-zee's cloaca. The pale crest turned and moved away.

When the officer was through with him, Soo-zee crawled back to the burrow. His cloaca was sore and sticky, but he was too tired to clean it. The officer had declared his undying devotion to Soo-zee and coupled with him three more times. Thank the Iridescent Spirit for dinka.

He slipped into his nest as quietly as he could. Little Dinka's nest was empty. A pair of eyes shone from Jee-ahn's nest.

"You stink, Soo-zee Wanabi."

Soo-zee didn't care.

The sun was almost at its zenith when Soo-zee finally dragged his tail to the yard for drill. Jee-ahn and Shi-ahn were already silently at work, the only sound that of their sticks smashing against each other. Another blue stood watching them.

"Who are you?" Soo-zee asked.

"Mee-kah Tamana, your new soldier. I got here late last night."

"Where is Goo-nah?" Soo-zee asked. "Where's Little Dinka?"

"Bah-kah and the porter have gone to look for them."

Jee-ahn knocked Shi-ahn's stick away and jumped on his back.

"Excellent, Inari" Shi-ahn chirped. "You are learning."

"Shouldn't we go look for them, too?" Soo-zee asked Mee-kah.

"Don't ask me," the recruit chirped. "I'm new here." Shi-ahn picked up his stick. "Again."

Jee-ahn lunged at him.

Bah-kah and Porter returned to camp that afternoon. Little Dinka looked tiny in Porter's oversized arms. The scout's lips and tongue were stained dark blue, his teeth worn down to nubs. A line of dark green blood lay congealed across his throat.

"Goo-nah," Bah-kah chirped, before anyone could ask. "Slit Little Dinka's throat then took his own life. Porter will have to go back and get him."

Soo-zee let his crest quiver openly. The loss of the Rohs had been bad enough, but this was worse. He wept for Little Dinka. He wept for Cho-ahn. Silently he cursed Goo-nah, hoping that if the Forever World existed, demons were taking turns with his hindquarters in the Underburrow.

Bah-kah knelt down in front of him. "We are soldiers. We fight on." But he put a claw tenderly on Soo-zee's crest.

No one stopped Soo-zee when he left the drill yard and headed toward the forever tree. He stared for a long time at the branch with his and Little Dinka's marks. Then he turned furiously on the marks of himself and the orange officer, scratching until the bark was raw and his claws were bloody and broken.

Jee-ahn came and got him when it was time for the cremation. "I'm sorry," he chirped. "I know how much he meant to you."

Soo-zee's crest started quivering again. "After they killed Cho-ahn I thought Little Dinka's would be the only mark with mine on the forever tree, and mine with his. He turned his eyes away from the tree. "Why is your mark not on here, Jee-ahn? Is there no one that you care for?"

"Blues don't carve the marks of lovers on trees. We carve the marks of those we have killed."

"Why in the Now World would you do that?"

"When you have killed someone, Soo-zee Wanabi, you will understand. Those you love leave you. But when you take a life, it is yours forever." He pointed at the tree. "Someday that tree will be full of the marks of enemies I have vanquished. And I will be bound to each of them for all time."

"You believe in the Forever World, then?"

"I believe it is the only world that matters, Soo-zee Wanabi. And now you must return to the drill yard so that we can send the spirits of Little Dinka and Goo-nah there."

"Aren't you coming?"

"I'll be there as soon as I can. I am ready to shed my skin."

As he returned to the yard, Soo-zee asked himself what he could have done differently to save Little Dinka.

Halfway back he turned back to look at the forever tree. He could no longer see his and Little Dinka's marks. All he could see was Jee-ahn, rubbing his white skin against the trunk.

By the time he got back to the yard, Porter had finished building a pyre big enough to accommodate Goo-nah and Little Dinka side by side.

"Where's Jee-ahn?" Bah-kah asked.

"Shedding."

"We'll wait," Shi-ahn chirped. "You'll see. He'll be back before sundown."

But the end of the day arrived and still Jee-ahn had not returned.

"That's odd," Shi-ahn chirped. "We blues shed our skins quickly."

"We should start without him," Mee-ahn chirped. "Spirits don't like to travel in the dark."

The sun dipped low in the sky. Porter lit the kindling. As the first duckwood log caught fire, Jee-ahn appeared. In the light of the flames, his new skin glowed a deep indigo.

The flames bit into Little Dinka's tail. An unappetizing smell filled the air—the scent of burning meat. How did they stand it in Burrow Town?

"Perhaps this will help," Jee-ahn held out a clawful of dinka seeds.

"Where did you get these?" Soo-zee asked.

Jee-ahn brought the seeds to Soo-zee's mouth. "You

are suffering. I know what that's like." Against his new skin, his teeth were blindingly white

Soo-zee ate the seeds. His tongue went numb and his jaw grew slack.

"More?" Jee-ahn asked. "Your teeth are almost as blue as my new skin."

Soo-zee nodded and Jee-ahn shoveled seeds into Soo-zee's mouth. Soon Soo-zee couldn't feel his hindquarters. He looked toward the fire and beheld the Iridescent Spirit. He saw Goonah and Little Dinka rise, holding holds. He felt no jealousy, no sorrow. All he felt was numb. "Why are you being so nice to me?" he asked.

"I saw you with that officer," Jee-ahn chirped. In the duckwood's white hot flames, his eyes were two pools of polished obsidian. His crest, no longer pale with old skin, shone deep purple. "Cho-ahn always insisted you could have become a Slayer had you been born in Burrow Town. But I think your weakness for pale crests and dinka makes you blind to what's right in front of you. For instance... did you know that Cho-ahn is a blue? He's only pale because he's albino. He sends you his regards, by the way, and is eagerly waiting to mount your branch on his wall."

"Cho-ahn's dead." Soo-zee's head felt as dense as a log of duckwood.

Jee-ahn clacked his tongue. "Dinka really does make one stupid. You don't honestly think His Grace would execute a Slayer do you?"

"A Slayer?" Soo-zee's chirps sounded like someone else's, dinka-slurred and slow.

"You've listened to too many of Little Dinka's stories. Slayers don't sneak in by night to kill His Grace's enemies. We find your weaknesses and let you kill yourselves."

"But you let Bah-kah…" Soo-zee's head was an entire tree now. He wasn't even sure he was chirping out loud.

"No—*you* let Bah-kah do it… you and the others. But I forgive you, Soo-zee Wanabi. You see, we Slayers have a saying: a blade is forged in fire. We are strong enough to bear any indignity, while you rebels care more for your own comfort and safety than in doing what is right. And that is why you will lose this war."

Soo-zee opened his mouth to protest, but Jee-ahn had the truth of it. Jee-ahn had borne his humiliation without complaint, while he, Soo-zee, had sat there and let Bah-kah abuse him and later blamed Jee-ahn for allowing it to happen. Shame burned a hole in his entrails, one that no amount of forgiveness could ever fill. He yearned for more dinka—for an end to the memory of Cho-ahn's betrayal and of Little Dinka limp in Porter's arms.

Jee-ahn looked at him with something that might have been pity. "While you were building the fire, I carved our marks in the forever tree."

But I've never submitted to you, Soo-zee thought.

"You haven't submitted yet," Jee-ahn answered, as if he'd heard him. "But you will. It is up to you, however, whether you submit to Cho-ahn or to me. Only one of us can claim the right to display a branch with your mark on it."

Behind them, the flames had diminished to embers.

"Choose now, Soo-zee Wanabi. Your time has come. Shall it be Cho-ahn?" Jee-ahn opened his left claw, in which a fresh pile of dinka seeds had magically appeared. "Or shall it be me?" He spread his right-side claws and Soo-zee saw just how sharp they were.

But the pangs of Soo-zee's conscience were sharper still. He fell to his knees and stretched out his throat to Jee-ahn.

JACKIE FUCHS

ABOUT THE AUTHOR

Jackie Fuchs is a Los Angeles-based writer and speaker whose work has been featured in *The Huffington Post, Listverse*, and *Boing Boing.*

As Jackie Fox, she was a member of the groundbreaking '70s rock band The Runaways.

She is not now—nor has she ever been—a lizard.

You can read more of Jackie's writing at https://jackiefox.net.